MUSTARD

Book III

Lessons From Old Souls

Story and Paintings by
Jessel Miller

Jessel Gallery

MUSTARD
LESSONS FROM OLD SOULS
Text and Illustrations Copyrights© 1999 Jessel Miller

ISBN: 0-9660381-5-0
Library of Congress Number: 99-095255

10 9 8 7 6 5 4 3 2 1
Editing by Carolynne Gamble
Typography, design and electronic prepress by Jim Scott
Printed by Tien Wah Press, Singapore

Publisher's Cataloging-in-Publication
(Provided by Quality Books)

Miller, Jessel.
    Mustard. Book III, Lessons from old souls /
    story and paintings by Jessel Miller. -- 1 st ed.
    p. cm. -- (Soft love, strong values; 3)
    LCCN: 99-095255
    ISBN: 0-9660381-5-0
    SUMMARY: In the Napa Valley, Mustard and River become parents of twins
Forest and Meadow, who are taught valuable lessons about nature, community
and love by their neighbors, family, teachers and Angel guides.

    1. Twins--Juvenile fiction. 2. Child rearing--Juvenile fiction.
3. Values--Juvenile fiction. 4. Napa Valley (Calif.)--Juvenile fiction.
    I. Title.

PZ7.M5554Muc 1999   [E]
        QBI99-883

MUSTARD, Lessons From Old Souls is dedicated to the Napa Valley Mustard Festival,
a non-profit community service organization and an official sponsor of this read-aloud
book for all ages. Each year, January through March, the Mustard Festival holds a
sensational season of events when wild mustard carpets the valley with splendid hues
of green and gold. Titled, "Mustard Miracles," the illustration on the cover has been
selected as the official 2000 7th Annual Napa Valley Mustard Festival poster.

Dedicated to Pat Summers and George Rothwell, – the master-minds behind the Mustard
Festival - for believing in Madame Mustard and for inspiring Jessel to walk through a
creative door she thought was locked.

Jessel Miller, the Jessel Gallery, and the Napa Valley Mustard Festival extend a special
thank you to our sponsors and producer for making the publication of this book possible:

Visa U.S.A. Inc.
Embassy Suites, Napa Valley
Napa Valley Wine Train
The Chronicle
ABC 7
Summers McCann, Inc. Public Relations (Producer of the Napa Valley Mustard Festival)

A portion of the proceeds from the sale of this book will benefit the
Napa Valley Mustard Festival. Web site: www.mustardfestival.org

This book is dedicated to

THE WORLD

All my life I have felt blessed every day by the lips that kiss and caress my cheek and by the gentle love that surrounds my heart. My prayer is for these books to bring tears to a tender heart and smiles to the lips of all who are touched by my humble truth.

I believe we are all here to share the gifts given to us as part of our universal birthright - and by following our highest path, we will reach nirvana.

*M*ustard and River lived on a bountiful four acre farm
in a home filled with welcoming objects like heart-rocks
gathered on their journeys to the sea . . . and the
comforting scent of fresh baked bread w a f t i n g in the air.

Their love was rich and royal, deep and trusting,
steeped in honesty, respect and compromise.

One cool winter night as winds howled against the windows
and a warm glow blazed in the stone fireplace,
Mustard fell into a d e e p s l e e p. She dreamed of
an Ancient Spirit who quietly told her she would
soon have two beautiful babies.

"These children are a divine and holy gift and

come to you as p u r e, c l e a r l i g h t.

They are o p e n t o r e c e i v e your wisdom and deep

understanding of all cultures, communities and colors.

Weave the texture and tapestry for these innocent souls,

forming and sculpting their inner and outer essence.

Stand beside them as they reflect your love

and grow up to continue your visions

throughout the universe."

In her dream, Mustard and her husband River
crossed a bridge made of stone
and a light shone before them.

A path led them to a quiet meadow
filled with blue birds and wildflowers.

And there before them stood . . .

Butterfly Spirit!

She hummed a soft lilting tune like ancient Indian flutes echoing over the hillsides.

"Time carries us down a river of life.

We create the ebbs and flows,

the gentle or vigorous currents.

Choose the peaceful, harmonious path.

Surround these spirits soon to come through you with

absolute, unconditional love,

and

enfold them in your bliss.

Accept the responsibility

of creating new life."

Mustard awoke and told River about her wonderful dream.
He smiled at her joy and laughed in his heart.

"Children are prayers answered," he said.

Just a few months later,
Mustard ran to River and told him of the news.
"We are going to be parents.
I am pregnant with twins," she announced!

River's heart began to race and they both cried.
"This is a blessed day. A miracle has happened."

That evening they walked to the top of their hill
and together they shouted to the universe,

"THANK YOU!"

The stars replied,

"YOU'RE WELCOME!"

Each day as the babies grew inside,
   Mustard nurtured her body with fruit from the orchards.
   Everything tasted sweeter and birds seemed to f l u t t e r
   inside her as she grew larger and happier with
   the thought of the new arrivals.

Morning glories spoke to her of wise choices.

"Drink lots of water.

Eat fresh grown vegetables and fruits,

a few raw nuts and seeds,

grains and legumes ~

a basic diet of honest foods.

Walk a gentle hill or meander a park.

Feed the soul, mind and body."

*M*ustard's visions e x p a n d e d and landed in her dreams each night.
A woman opened her bird cage and set her sweet doves free.

"I release this most precious gift to the world," she said.

"I bless and set them free."

"Fear not," whispered the doves as they f l e w o f f ·

"We will carry you in our hearts forever."

Mustard awoke knowing that she must
    let her children go right from the start.
    For in letting go, she accepted
    the freedom and individuality of her unborn children.

At sunrise on a crisp fall day, two beautiful babies were born.
Mustard & River wrapped their arms around New Life
and named them Forest and Meadow.

Both cooed and cuddled
close to their parents and slept soundly.
Together they grew in their curiosity and wisdom ~
surrounded safely by soft love and strong values.

At a Baby Blessing to welcome the new spirits,
the family gathered in a circle and said,

"We ask the wind to carry our seeds

on a protected journey into the world

and plant them into rich soil.

We ask the rain to water the earth,

the sun to share its light,

and the world to keep them safe and secure.

We ask ALL to answer our prayers.

Inspire us to breathe life into these yearning arms

and caress their lips

with a deep and gentle kiss."

The whole community rejoiced.

As they grew, Mustard and River
spent hours sharing joyous moments,
watching and teaching their children
from a knowledge deep in their hearts.

FAMILY

is a word

which brings all of us

together

in a

universal connection.

One rainy day,
Meadow and Forest were playing and watching the flowers
welcome the weather.

Father Rain t h u n d e r e d from the clouds,

"Like the trees that grow in the forest of life,

our bodies must be ONE with nature

to nurture the life rings.

B r e a t h e the light force air

and

d r i n k the earthly gift of water.

Nature holds all the secrets,

all the answers

all the patterns

all the colors

all the cures."

It was the first time they felt r a i n d r o p s upon their cheeks
and they ran and j u m p e d in puddles for as long as they liked.

"Nature is whimsical, wonderful and wise."

Ruby was a dear neighbor who would sit with the children
for hours telling stories of her heritage.
She spent her days in the garden and the kitchen, and
loved to bake and entertain.

Thus began the *lessons from old souls* . . .

Ruby always made special treats for the children
and they rushed to her farm singing out,

"Ruby, Ruby you are our friend!

Ruby, Ruby our love will never end."

Ruby treasured the sound of their sweet voices calling
and sang out to them in return,

"Meadow and Forest come to me.

Always f u l l o f f u n a n d g l e e .

We are friends and I am sure

My love for you is s w e e t a n d p u r e ."

$\mathcal{R}$uby gathered all the neighborhood children
and spoke to them softly,

"We are all one world, each unique and different,

yet all running in the same race,

the Human Race.

Accept and respect each other

every single day, all along the way,"

she would sing.

The children felt blessed by her kindness and understanding.

$\mathcal{F}$orest and Meadow adored their grandparents,
aunts, uncles, and family friends.
They loved to listen to stories of long ago.
They learned to honor the elders
who through their years of life experience and
devotion to children,
returned the sum ten fold and beyond.

Each person has a story to tell and challenges to overcome,

best done with a positive attitude.

The children sat nestled in graceful arms and heard
important lessons of the journeys, trials and
tribulations of these souls who came before them.

$\mathcal{P}$apa taught them to s l o w d o w n along the path.

"Watch the signs and read the signals,

and the answers will unfold," he said.

"Follow your instincts.

Know when to stop.

You have a choice at every turn.

Be wise and choose the calmest road.

Pause to think before you act,

and consider the effect

with every choice."

"From the fish in the sea,

to the stars in the sky,

the air we b r e a t h e

and

the earth beneath our feet,

Be benevolent

stewards

and

guardians

of this

planet."

As their children grew older, River and Mustard
believed they were ready to travel the world.

On their first journey abroad the family stayed in a quaint village.
The people looked different and customs were unfamiliar.
Their parents taught them to honor the uniqueness of others.
Ruby came to mind.

One extraordinary day,
Grand Man Person danced around Meadow and said,

"Peace is a state of mind. Stay in it.

Adore one another.

Be a good universal neighbor.

Have faith in your ability to forgive and grow

from the challenges in your life.

To love and honor yourself

is to love and honor others."

$\mathscr{A}$ few years later they traveled to another country.

Wild Wind Woman blew in and wrapped
Forest in a brocade robe so fine and

w h i s p e r e d ,

"Wealth is not what you have.

Wealth is who you are

and

y o u

are a treasure beyond money.

To be rich in spirit is true wealth."

Wealth is not what you have

Wealth is who you are and you
are a treasure beyond
money

Mustard and River marveled how their curious children
welcomed new cultures, clothing, words and foods.

Before their very eyes these sweet creations grew and
discovered that life is a continual process.

Changing ~ rearranging

flexing ~ growing

flowing ~ soaring

relaxing

and

enjoying

the

ride.

On another exciting trip
      the Great Grandmother of the Community told them …

"We are equal in the eyes of all who have come before us.

We are born naked and we all start with love.

We all have hardships to overcome,

yet if we base our lives in one simple place in our hearts ~

giving, sharing, creating, pursuing, expressing,

developing, studying, inventing

~

whatever the desire

will bring the greatest gifts of all

~

a contented soul and a calm spirit."

One Spring the family ventured to a gentle land
  where people wore plain clothes
  and lived without electricity.
  All had beautiful gardens and traveled by horse and carriage.

Their words were kind and simple:

"Touching

all things by hand

is the best way

to stay in contact

with

Mother Earth

and

Father Time."

Mustard, River, Meadow and Forest
  listened to the laughter of the children playing
  as the sun sank into the dusk.
  Such a sweet and honest joy.

When Forest and Meadow turned eighteen,
they had a ceremony for their coming of age.

The whole town came out to celebrate and the children
gave them gifts they had made in honor of this day.

Old Ancient Father said,

"You are the greatest work of art.

Create your beam of Light.

Glow a warmth of honesty and beauty.

Share the gift of your grace with this planet.

The glow will spread a thousand lights

to the universes beyond.

Honor your gifts, talents and attributes,

and trust yourself and your positive choices.

You hold the key to the

J O Y

of future generations.

As students today, you now become

the teachers of tomorrow."

*F*orest stepped forward and declared,

"From our grandparents, parents, family, friends, teachers and
Angel guides, we have been taught many *lessons from old souls*.

We each have wrong and right,
left and right, bad and good, darkness and light.

We have come to understand that we are spirits of divine light
grown in the soil of
VALUES AND VIRTUES.
Through stormy times filled with difficult and mighty experiences,
to smooth and silky seas, we have sailed beside you
safely in your loving arms.

From atop mountains you have taught us to listen to the winds
whisper ancient lessons of kinship to the land and animals.

We have learned that we must choose the focus
and go to the place of our deepest voice of love ~
and
L I S T E N."

$\mathcal{M}$eadow continued . . .

"In all our travels we have discovered that

WISDOM and TRUTH

are the same everywhere and at the center of each being is a

seed that began as something

PERFECT AND BEAUTIFUL.

Each day we are given a new morning.

We choose what best nurtures our inner child

and those around us.

You have given us the knowledge to choose

WISELY and SLOWLY.

We stand as humankind ready to light the way

for future generations

passing on our greatest lessons as you have done for us.

We open our hearts, choose with clear intent,

respect others and above all,

L I V E

L O V E."

Listen to the voice of Love

Jessel Miller

Jessel Miller was born in a small town in northern Ontario, Canada in 1949. Her father was a Country Doctor/Artist and Mom was the festive Singer, Poet and Entertainer in the family. Jessel was an extremely shy and withdrawn child.

Timmins was a safe and beautiful environment and had a grace and respect surrounding the community. Creativity was nurtured in the schools and Jessel's mother directed Jessel to expressive classes to bring her out of her shell. Music, dance and art were her favorites and she blossomed with each new lesson.

In 1965 the family moved to Florida and life changed completely. Jessel returned to her creative core to protect her shy center and spent hours painting in her room. Her focus from that time forth was directed towards fine art, writing, music and dance. To this day she has continued her love of art and has shared her gifts with the community as she watched her parents do.

Jessel moved to Oakland, California in 1971 after graduating from the University of Florida with a degree in Fine Art and a minor in Museum Directorship and English. Her first break came in 1980 with a one person show at the San Francisco Museum of Modern Art. Jessel had focused on faces for many years and this exhibition was entitled, "Bay Area Personalities." Maya Angelou, Herb Caen, Louise Davies, Melvin Belli and Dianne Feinstein were a few of the 25 personalities she painted for a successful and entertaining watercolor portrait show.

Napa had always reminded Jessel of her small town roots, so in 1984 she picked up her life and opened the Jessel Gallery in Napa, California. It all began with 300 square feet and 30 artists and 15 years later, the gallery is 9000 square feet exhibiting 300 artists.

The heart and soul of the MUSTARD triology reflects her childhood and the series is filled with lessons of love and kindness. Through writing and art, her dream is to carry the treasures received from her fortunate upbringing, out into the world.

For more information about gifts and products from the Mustard Trilogy, order directly from:

Jessel Gallery   1019 Atlas Peak Road   Napa, California 94558
888-702-6323 • voice   707-257-2396 • fax
email: jessel@napanet.net   Web site: www.jesselgallery.com

SELECTED PRINTS FROM EACH BOOK ARE AVAILABLE